# CONTEMPORARY MUSICIANS
## AND THEIR MUSIC ™

# Switchfoot

**Robert Zimmerman**

The Rosen Publishing Group, Inc., New York

Published in 2007 by The Rosen Publishing Group, Inc.
29 East 21st Street, New York, NY 10010

First Edition

**Library of Congress Cataloging-in-Publication Data**

Zimmerman, Robert K.
Switchfoot/Robert Zimmerman.—1st ed.
    p. cm.—(Contemporary musicians and their music)
Includes discography, bibliographical references, and index.
ISBN 1-4042-0709-0 (library binding)
1. Switchfoot (Musical group)—Juvenile literature. 2. Rock groups—California—Juvenile literature. 3. Christian rock music—Juvenile literature. 4. Rock musicians—California—Biography—Juvenile literature. I. Title. II. Series.
ML3930.S99Z56 2007
782.42166092'2—dc22

                                                                2005033266

*Manufactured in Malaysia*

**On the cover:** The members of Switchfoot soak up the sun at Santa Monica Pier. Shown from left are Jerome Fontamillas, Chad Butler, Tim Foreman, Jon Foreman, and Andrew Shirley.

# Contents

# Introduction

In June 2004, a new song burst onto *Billboard* magazine's chart of top 100 hits. "Meant to Live" was a rock anthem with fierce guitar riffs, heartfelt vocals, and a sing-along chorus, but it was different from most rock music on the charts. Instead of focusing on love, dancing, having fun, or being cool, "Meant to Live" asked listeners to think again about their lives and to demand more of themselves.

The song was written and performed by Switchfoot, one of the most exciting bands in

Switchfoot singer and guitarist Jon Foreman performs in 2004 at Madison Square Garden, the legendary sports arena in New York City.

rock music today. In addition to selling thousands of records, their music has been used in television shows and movies. They have appeared on MTV and in the pages of *Entertainment Weekly*, and they have worked with many of the superstars of the music business. But perhaps their biggest accomplishment is that they have become successful while remaining true to their fans and true to their own strong ideals. From the beginning to the present, Switchfoot has emphasized a positive message: Believe in yourself, help others, and try to make the world a better place.

To find success without sacrificing what they believed in was not easy. After all, when the band was first starting out, they had no idea how far their music would take them, or what kinds of obstacles they would encounter along the way. It took years of patience, hard work, and faith before other people began to appreciate their music. By now, the secret is out: Switchfoot is a band with great ideas and even better songs. Their unique music is now loved by music fans all over the globe.

# Chapter One

# The Early Days

**S**witchfoot has five members: Jon Foreman on guitar and vocals; his brother, Tim Foreman, on bass; Chad Butler on drums; Jerome Fontamillas on keyboards; and Andrew Shirley on guitar. But when the band first got together in San Diego, California, in the 1990s, there were only three: Jon, Tim, and Chad.

Jon Foreman was born on October 22, 1976, in San Bernardino, California. Tim was born two years later, on August 15, 1978. Their mother is an artist and art teacher, while their father is a pastor. Jon and Tim's interest in music surfaced when they were very young. In an interview on the Web site Jesusfreakhideout.com, Jon says, "My brother and I have been playing music together as long as I can remember." In the same interview, Tim recalls one

Switchfoot bassist Tim Foreman provides backup vocals during a 2004 concert in Atlanta, Georgia. Tim is the youngest member of the band. He names Paul McCartney of the Beatles as the biggest influence on his bass playing.

of the first albums he ever heard, *The Joshua Tree* by Irish band U2. In 1987, when Tim was nine, that album went to number one on the charts and won a Grammy for Album of the Year. It was an unusual and groundbreaking record for the time, containing heartfelt music and very sincere lyrics. Although he was very young, Tim remembers being blown away by the album. The album inspired him to take up the bass in fifth grade. Little did he know that one day he would meet his hero, U2's Bono!

## Surf Music

As teenagers, Jon and Tim spent half their time surfing in the crystal blue Pacific Ocean and the other half making music.

Jon Foreman is a gifted and award-winning musician. In 2001, he received the Les Paul Horizon Award as the music industry's most promising up-and-coming guitarist. But Jon's real judges are his loyal fans: he has performed live for more than 1.5 million people!

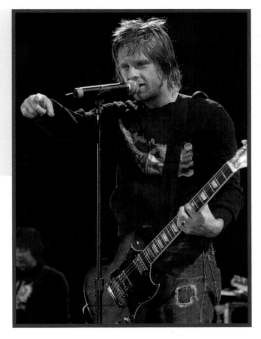

Jon played in a few different bands, including one that covered songs by '70s rockers Led Zeppelin, best known for their hit "Stairway to Heaven." Jon started college at the University of California, San Diego (UCSD), which had one of the best surfing teams in the country. Of course, Jon signed up for the team, along with a high school friend of his, Chad Butler.

Chad is a couple of years older than Jon. He was born March 24, 1974, in Amsterdam, the Netherlands. Like Jon and Tim, Chad is the son of a pastor. (His father, Chuck Butler, is also a Christian musician.) Chad's family moved to San Diego, where he learned to surf, eventually becoming good enough to make some extra money giving lessons in his spare time. Although,

Switchfoot drummer Chad Butler wears shades to protect himself from the sun at an outdoor concert in September 2005. Chad is one of the founding members of the band, which formed in 1996 in San Diego, California.

like Jon and Tim, Chad excelled at surfing, the friends really connected through music.

Jon, Tim, and Chad formed Switchfoot while Tim was still attending San Dieguito High School, and Jon and Chad were in college at UCSD. The band took their name from an unusual and tricky surfing move. A "switchfoot" is when you change the foot you are leading with while you are riding a wave. According to Jon, the move was popular back in the 1970s, but nowadays it's considered pretty goofy—you wouldn't do a switchfoot to impress your friends, you would do it to make them laugh. But the name "Switchfoot" also has a deeper meaning for the band. It means a change of direction, a reorientation, a decision to do things differently and turn your life around. In this sense, "Switchfoot" was the perfect name for a band interested in making positive changes in their lives and the lives of their fans.

## Enter Charlie Peacock

The Switchfoot trio—Jon, Tim, and Chad—rehearsed like crazy and eventually started touring. They played in sweaty rock clubs and churches, coffee shops and bars, and any other venue that would have them. They made demo tapes of their music and sold them for just a buck at their shows. After about twenty performances, a man named Charlie Peacock signed them to his independent record label, Re:Think Records.

Re:Think Records was a perfect fit for a band whose main purpose was getting its listeners to rethink their lives. Charlie Peacock is a talented singer and songwriter who produces innovative and accessible spiritual music. His songs have been recorded by such Christian music stars as dc Talk and Amy Grant. Switchfoot is also a Christian band, although they feel a bit uncomfortable with the idea that there is such a specific kind of music as "Christian music." Jon has been quoted in numerous sources as saying the band is "Christian by faith, not by genre." In other words, he believes that the religious beliefs of the band shape the ideas of the music but do not define them as a

Charlie Peacock has been a popular figure in Christian music for more than twenty years. In addition to his success as a musician and music producer, Charlie is also an accomplished author. The band considers Charlie an enormous influence—on both their music and their spirituality.

particular kind of music or sound.

They do not want to preach to their audience. Instead, they want to let their Christian values of tolerance, modesty, and love for others shine through in their music and reach a larger number of people than just Christian rock fans.

Besides this spiritual connection, there were many other reasons that Switchfoot and Charlie Peacock were a good match. Peacock's experience in the music business would help Switchfoot turn their raw sound into something more professional. Also, he could work as a producer on their records. The producer of a record is the person responsible for supervising the recording process. Like the conductor of a symphony orchestra, the producer is responsible for shaping the sound as a whole. Each musician may be a master of his or her instrument, but the result will be chaotic if there is not one person who can help put the pieces together in the studio.

There were also advantages to working with Re:Think records. As an independent record label rather than a huge corporation, they were used to working with young bands and encouraging them to experiment and develop their sound. Independent record labels do not always have to produce big hits that fit into the latest trends. Because of their small size, they have the opportunity to produce more unique kinds of music.

## The First Record

Switchfoot recorded their debut record, *The Legend of Chin*, in a few weeks in 1997. The band members were still quite young—in fact, the record was released the day before Tim graduated from high school. Due to their youth and the fact that the record was recorded quickly, it has a slightly rough sound. Still, with the help of their producer and their record label, they managed to produce a very successful album.

With sounds ranging from alternative pop to hard rock, *The Legend of Chin* features standout tracks like "Bomb," which is about fighting your way out of depression and apathy. Another

13

highlight is "Chem 6a," about the mind-numbing quality of television and not wanting to do anything with your life. Throughout, the album deals with depression and struggles, while also providing a consistent message of hope. It takes its unusual name from a friend of the band, Willis Chin.

"We called our album 'The Legend of Chin' out of respect for our friend back in San Diego," explained Chad in an interview with *Christianity Today* magazine. "He's such a great guy. A real smiler, too. The kind of guy who always has his chin up!" Jon described Willis as being one of his heroes: "He's so real and so consistent in living out his faith. He's no fake. And that's what we hope our album is all about—about being real, no matter what the situation or circumstance." Tim agreed: "We are trying to show people where true hope is found, and Willis knows exactly where his hope is found." The song "Ode to Chin" helps spread the message of which Willis Chin is the living example.

The band used photos of Willis for their album art, including photos of him as a baby, in his football uniform, and at the prom. "When Willis's mom saw the CD she couldn't figure it out," Chad told *Christianity Today*. "She kept asking him, 'Why are all these pictures of you in here?' And Willis is like, 'I don't know, Mom!' Actually, both his mom and dad think it's all pretty funny . . . All kidding aside, though, Willis just means a lot to us and that's why we did it." Willis Chin even appears in almost all of the band's music videos. Now, almost ten years after Switchfoot recorded an album in his honor, Willis plays in a band called Movement Oust and sometimes leads worship at Calvary Chapel North Coast, a church in San Diego.

## Chapter Two

# A New Member Joins the Band

**T**he *Legend of Chin* established Switchfoot as a major player in the San Diego music scene. In 1997, they were awarded the ASCAP (American Society of Composers, Authors and Publishers) San Diego award for Best New Artist. In 1999, they released their second album, *New Way to Be Human*, which was even more successful than their first release. The most popular song on the album was the title track. It revisited a common Switchfoot theme: the emptiness of modern life and how to turn your back on shallow trends to search for deeper meaning.

With an award under their belt, their new album selling well, and their concerts selling out, Switchfoot was no longer just a local rock band with a Christian twist. They were closer than ever

Switchfoot (from left, Chad, Jon, Tim, and Jerome) arrive at the 2004 American Music Awards in Los Angeles, California. No longer an up-and-coming act, the band was invited to the awards ceremony to present the award for Contemporary Inspirational Music. Other presenters at the show included Clay Aiken, Kelly Clarkson, and tennis superstars Venus and Serena Williams.

to mainstream success. Looking for a way to fine-tune their sound, Switchfoot found the perfect solution in Jerome Fontamillas, who became the fourth member of the band. Jerome was born in the Philippines but grew up in the United States. His parents made him take piano lessons when he was young, and although he hated it at first, he soon caught the music bug. Jerome's parents supported his plans to become a musician and encouraged him to follow his dream. In high school, Jerome switched to bass and guitar, since those were the "cool" instruments. Later, he played bass and guitar with a band called Fold Zandura, but that band broke up in 2000. Jerome was also in Mortal, an influential Christian band that had a heavy, electronic sound.

Jerome had been friends with Switchfoot for some time and had several years of experience as a musician. When he called up Switchfoot and asked if they needed a keyboard player, the answer was a big "yes." Jerome became an essential part of the Switchfoot team. In addition to keyboards, Jerome could also play rhythm guitar, keeping the band's chords in line and providing an anchor for the music.

In fact, just about the only thing that Jerome couldn't do with Switchfoot was surf. Now that he is a member of the band, he is starting to get the hang of it, but he still hasn't mastered the

Jerome Fontamillas is Switchfoot's keyboard player. He was born in the Philippines, a country made up of over 7,000 islands located off the coast of Southeast Asia. Besides playing keyboards and rhythm guitar, he also sometimes performs backup vocals.

move after which the band is named. He told *Blender* magazine, "I've been able to do the move only while already underwater—that is, after I've fallen off the board."

## *Learning to Breathe*

Soon after Jerome joined, the band recorded their third album, *Learning to Breathe*. Although *Learning to Breathe* was still an independent record, in many ways it was Switchfoot's breakthrough album. The band had not yet built a wide fan base outside the Christian music community and their San Diego roots, but *Learning to Breathe* grabbed the attention of influential people in the music world. A mark of the record's success was a Grammy nomination for Best Rock Gospel Album in 2001. This was a huge honor, as Grammys are the music industry's most coveted awards.

*Learning to Breathe*, like *The Legend of Chin* and *New Way to Be Human*, asks listeners to consider new paths in their lives and to tune out the constant pop-culture buzz of everyday life. The cleverly titled song "Poparazzi" (a pun on the word "paparazzi," meaning photographers who follow celebrities around trying to take their pictures) reiterates Switchfoot's theme of searching for a life that's more meaningful than the life idealized by television, movies, and pop songs. The album also included the song "Dare You to Move." This song turned out to be one of their most popular hits for many years to come. The lyrics encourage listeners to take a leap of faith and try something new and bold with their lives. Switchfoot had certainly taken their own advice, starting as a small rock band and becoming a nationally recognized Christian music act. The band's powerful words and sound were finding new fans all over the world.

# Chapter Three

# Breaking Through

**S**witchfoot toured relentlessly to promote *Learning to Breathe*, playing small rock clubs in towns across America. At the height of their tour, Switchfoot played more than 150 shows in a year. Reaching out to an international audience, they traveled to England to play a show in London. Despite the crazy schedule, they still made time for their other passion: surfing. In an interview with the Web site Vox Online, Jon remembered one time they took it too far. "We were playing in London, and we heard from someone that there was this great swell over in France, and we just had to get to it. So, we spent basically all of our money to get over there and surf and get back. We had nothing when we got back, so we actually ended up sleeping in the streets."

Switchfoot became known for their awesome live perform-ances. Maybe that's because they treat their audience as a part of the show just as important as the band itself. As Jon explained in an interview with the Web site musicOMH.com, "We have always taken the approach that we as the band and the audience are just two parts of the same thing. We're not up on stage taking ourselves too seriously, we're just part of the whole."

## Enter Mandy Moore

In addition to their many loyal fans around the country, it turned out that Switchfoot had a well-known fan within the music business: pop princess Mandy Moore. Moore was known for her hit song "Candy" and her role as a popular mean girl in the movie *The Princess Diaries*. While Switchfoot was touring in support of *Learning to Breathe*, Mandy was working on a new movie called *A Walk to Remember*. The movie was about a preacher's daughter who falls in love with a troubled, popular boy played by Shane West. She helps him become a better, stronger, and kinder person.

The theme of *A Walk to Remember* matched Switchfoot's message of hope, self-reliance, and positive change. Mandy's manager, Jon Leshay of Storefront Entertainment, had heard Switchfoot's music through a college friend. He instantly wanted

Mandy Moore and Shane West play a couple that fall in love in the movie *A Walk to Remember*. In addition to this film, Shane has played a doctor on the television drama *E.R.*, while Mandy has starred in movies including *Saved!* and *How to Deal*.

them to participate in the movie. Mandy was a big fan, too, and was excited to include the band on the soundtrack. In all, Jon and Switchfoot contributed five songs to the soundtrack, including a duet between Mandy and Jon entitled "Someday We'll Know." The other songs were "Learning to Breathe" (originally on the album of the same name), "You," "Only Hope," and the anthem "Dare You to Move." This last song had three lives: In addition to being featured on the album *Learning to Breathe*, then in *A Walk to Remember*, "Dare You to Move" would soon become a big hit on Switchfoot's album *The Beautiful Letdown*.

The *A Walk to Remember* soundtrack was a surprise hit, selling over a million copies. The album also gave Switchfoot the crossover appeal they had lacked. Now it wasn't just the Christian music scene that was picking up Switchfoot songs, but mainstream radio.

The soundtrack also resulted in another major change for the band. Jon Leshay would be around to usher Switchfoot into the big leagues. He became their manager after the movie. The manager handles the business side of things, such as booking concerts and handling contracts. These may not be so important for a small-time act, but it's important for a highly successful band to have a manager so they can focus on their music.

## An Expanding Audience

At about the same time that they appeared on the *A Walk to Remember* soundtrack, Switchfoot was finding yet another way

## CROSSOVER

Many bands are popular among fans of a particular kind of music, such as country or heavy metal, but almost unknown to the broad mass of radio listeners. Similarly, many Christian bands, like Switchfoot, find it difficult to cross over into the mainstream. Some other popular bands who started out with a religious following but found crossover success are Creed, Third Day, and Evanescence.

A highlight of any Switchfoot concert is the interaction between the fans and the band. Above, Jon sings surrounded by a crowd of adoring fans in Sunrise, Florida, during the 2004 Jingle Ball concert.

to reach a big mainstream audience: television. Switchfoot's songs were featured on episodes of a number of popular shows, such as *Dawson's Creek*, *Felicity*, and *Party of Five*. Having their music played on television helped Switchfoot to expand their fan base, preparing them for even greater success in the future. Soon, they would go on to be featured on other television shows, including *One Tree Hill*, *Charmed*, and *Summerland*, and the international soundtrack of the blockbuster movie *Spider-Man 2*.

Sometimes, however, their songs were used for TV shows in ways that didn't quite fit with the themes of the music. "The context in which the songs are used can be pretty funny," Jon Foreman said in a band press release. "I remember writing a song about spiritual longing and then seeing it played back during a hot-tub scene on some show." Jon was referring to the song "You," Switchfoot's soulful song about finding meaning through a higher power. It had ended up being played on the teen drama *Dawson's Creek*.

While the band's career was taking off, there were other big events going on for the band members that had nothing to do with music. Jon Foreman married his wife, Emily, in January 2002. Bassist Tim Foreman married his wife, Andrea, in spring 2001 (they now have a baby boy, Jack). Also in spring 2001, Chad Butler and his wife, Tina, had a son, Evan. Three years later they had another son, Dylan. Chad says it's hard to be on the road all the time and away from his family. He is away on tour for weeks at a time, but says that he appreciates every moment he can spend with his family.

# Chapter Four

# A Platinum Record

**S**witchfoot's songs on the *A Walk to Remember* soundtrack got the attention of Columbia Records, a major record label that has worked with superstars such as Jessica Simpson, Beyoncé, Bob Dylan, Prince, Nas, and System of a Down. Columbia approached Switchfoot about recording for them, and the deal worked out great for the band. Being picked up by Columbia meant much more publicity, marketing, and support for their music. Switchfoot didn't waste any time recording their next release, *The Beautiful Letdown*. In fact, they recorded it from start to finish in just seventeen days. Those seventeen days would turn out to be some of the most important of their lives. *The Beautiful Letdown* would prove that Switchfoot was no longer an underground phenomenon, but had become a full-blown sensation.

During the time that they were recording, though, there were still quite a few people in the music business who had never heard of Switchfoot. According to MTV News, Jon Foreman had an embarrassing moment when he was first recording tracks for *The Beautiful Letdown*. He reached the building where he was supposed to meet his producer, Jack Joseph Puig. But Jon didn't have a room number, and he found himself wandering the halls, looking for the studio where he was scheduled to record. Seeing a sign on a door saying "Closed Session," Jon thought that might be the right room. So he walked right in, and found himself smack in the middle of a recording session with the alternative rock supergroup Radiohead. Momentarily baffled, Jon thought maybe the guys from Radiohead were there to sit in on a Switchfoot session. He figured out he was in the wrong place when lead singer Thom Yorke said, "I don't mean to be an idiot, but if you could please leave? It's a private studio." Jon, terribly embarrassed, quickly left, but he has such a sense of humor about the incident that he's told the story several times.

Switchfoot performs at the Avalon Hollywood, a large dance and rock club in Los Angeles, California. The concert was the first show of the band's 2004 American tour. From left are Jon, Andrew, and Tim. Andrew Shirley began touring with the band in 2003 and officially became a member in 2005.

# The First Single

The song "Meant to Live" was released as the first single off the album in 2003. However, it didn't become an instant hit. Band manager Jon Leshay chose a slow and steady path of marketing. Rather than hype up the band, bombarding every radio station with pressure to play Switchfoot's songs, Leshay decided to introduce their sound gradually. He wanted to simply put the music out there and let it speak for itself. This was a good strategy. Many albums and songs may be wildly successful for the first few weeks after they are released and then fizzle out quickly, leaving the band overexposed and soon forgotten. Switchfoot was looking at the long run and was committed to making music for many years to come. The band had always had a word-of-mouth following, and that's the way they preferred it. They wanted to make an album that friends would pass on to their friends, not something that would just be the hit song of the summer.

It was a gamble, but it paid off. As Switchfoot toured relentlessly around the country, radio stations in the towns where they played began picking up the song "Meant to Live." When sales climbed to 150,000, the band was surprised at how well the album was selling. Still, they had little idea of what would happen next. In December 2003, the album went gold, after selling 500,000 copies. Those numbers were large enough to make the executives at Columbia Records take notice. Columbia approved larger budgets for promoting the album and for making videos, which are a crucial element to success for today's musicians. With this final push, the album sold more than 1 million copies by April 2004, to become a certified platinum record.

## Shooting Up the Charts

"Meant to Live" went on to crack the Top 10 on the Billboard Modern Rock charts and spent over a year getting play on the radio—a long life even for a hit single. The song "Dare You to Move" got lots of airplay as well. The video for "Meant to Live" reached the Top 20 on MTV, MTV2, and VH1. Switchfoot was booked on many TV shows, including *The Tonight Show with Jay Leno*, the *Late Show with David Letterman*, *Late Night with Conan O'Brien*, *Last Call with Carson Daly*, CBS's *The Late Late Show with Craig Kilborn*, and ABC's *Jimmy Kimmel Live*. As Switchfoot expanded their touring, kicking off a national tour in October 2004, their audience grew even more. The enthusiasm that the band generated at their concerts was contagious. Switchfoot was taking the music scene by storm.

Switchfoot ended 2004 at number 40 on the Billboard album chart, after peaking at number 16. They also did well on the contemporary Christian charts, showing that while they had crossed over to the mainstream, they were still hanging on to their roots. Most important to the band, they had been able to find success without compromising their unique point of view. When all was said and done, Switchfoot had sold over 2.5 million copies of *The Beautiful Letdown* and toured the country four times to support it.

# GOLD RECORD

The gold record was first given as a publicity stunt in 1941 to a jazz band leader named Glen Miller, whose song "Chattanooga Choo Choo" sold 1 million copies. His record company took one of the records and sprayed it with gold paint. In 1958, the Recording Industry Association of America (RIAA) made the gold record an official award. To be certified gold, a record must sell at least 500,000 copies. The next level up from a gold record is a platinum record, when a record sells 1 million copies. A record that sells 2 million copies is double platinum. In 1999, the RIAA added a diamond record, for recordings that sell 10 million copies or more. The musician with the most gold, platinum, and double-platinum records is Elvis Presley, with 147.

Switchfoot accepts the award for Rock/Contemporary Album of the Year for *The Beautiful Letdown* at the 2004 Gospel Music Association Awards. The band also received awards for Rock Song of the Year ("Ammunition") and Rock/Contemporary Song of the Year ("Meant to Live").

While *The Beautiful Letdown* was still hot on the charts, Switchfoot released a live-music DVD entitled *Live in San Diego*. The DVD featured a live concert recorded at the punk-rock venue Soma in San Diego. For fans who couldn't make it to the Switchfoot shows, or for those who just couldn't get enough of Switchfoot's music, the DVD was a way to have a Switchfoot concert on hand whenever they wanted one.

# Chapter Five

# Helping Others

Their unexpected success meant many things for Switchfoot. Beyond the financial rewards, it gave them the opportunity to meet their heroes and the chance to speak out on issues that are important to them. For example, they had the opportunity to work with one of the band's heroes, U2's lead singer Bono, on global political issues.

Switchfoot has long admired Bono for his music, his faith, and his unwavering commitment to using his fame to help others. So when Switchfoot was invited to participate in the Debt, AIDS, Trade, Africa (DATA) summit in Nashville in December 2002, they were honored. (DATA is an organization founded by Bono to raise awareness about critical issues facing Africa.) Jon Foreman

Switchfoot celebrated the release of its fifth album, *Nothing Is Sound*, with a free concert in Santa Monica, California. At the show, the band collected donations to help victims of Hurricane Katrina, the devastating storm that hit the U.S. Gulf Coast in August 2005.

said listening to Bono speak was a "life-changing experience." When he got the chance to meet Bono, he handed him forty dollars in cash. "I told him I owed it to him for sneaking into a U2 show in London a couple of years ago," he says in a band press release. "He laughed and told me he did the same thing when he was younger."

Another interesting project that Switchfoot took on was to travel to South Africa to record the Kuyasa Kids, a children's choir in the capital city of Cape Town. The band has released a

CD of the children's music and plans to donate the proceeds to the community there.

More recently, Switchfoot threw a charity event of its own. The Switchfoot Bro-Am was a surf contest that took place in March 2005. Four surfing teams competed to win, but there was a catch—they had to ride one wave normally and the other one switchfoot. The event also included a benefit concert to raise money for Care House, a nonprofit group that serves teens in crisis throughout San Diego. The homeless teenagers who live in Care House were given free shoes, clothes, surfing lessons, surfboards, guitar lessons, and guitars. Switchfoot, true to form, was encouraging the kids to believe in themselves and dream that life could be better.

## It's All About the Fans

In addition to helping others less fortunate than themselves, Switchfoot has continued to make time for their fans. According to *Entertainment Weekly*, one major fan e-mailed the band to ask if they could help him propose to his girlfriend. Switchfoot thought it sounded like fun and agreed to help out. They even enlisted a posh jewelry store to donate the engagement ring! After playing a concert at a huge amphitheater in a New Jersey

Jon Foreman poses for a picture with fans in Sydney, Australia, in September 2005. Unfortunately for the young ladies in the crowd, Jon's wedding band is clearly visible on the ring finger of his left hand.

amusement park, Switchfoot met the fan and his girlfriend backstage. She had no idea what was coming next.

At first Switchfoot pretended that they were just signing autographs. Then Jon stepped in. "She seems like a nice girl. What are you waiting for?" he asked the boyfriend. With that, the lucky guy produced the diamond ring and popped the question. To everyone's relief, she said yes.

Another fan the band helped out was a teenager from Alabama who was battling cancer. His mother, knowing how much he loved Switchfoot's music, called the band's concert promoter to try to get some autographs for her son. The promoter contacted Switchfoot, and the band decided to visit the boy before their performance in town. After meeting them, he was able to attend the concert in his wheelchair. Seeing his determination to beat the disease, Switchfoot must have found new meaning in their song "Meant to Live."

## Making a New Album

While they were on tour promoting *The Beautiful Letdown*, Switchfoot wrote many new songs, trying them out on the fans who attended their concerts. The band believes that testing out songs on the road is the best way to see what's hot and what's not. "You know if a song is working or not when you step onstage and play it," Tim told MTV News. Jon added, "In many ways, our crowds every night would help us produce the songs. You can tell. You look in their eyes and you can tell if a chorus is working or not." They also tested out newcomer Andrew Shirley, who toured the country with Switchfoot playing guitar and who is now an official Switchfoot member.

Switchfoot included some of the material written during *The Beautiful Letdown* tour on their latest album, *Nothing Is Sound*, which was released on September 13, 2005. After only a week on the shelves, the album had already reached number 3 on the Billboard Top 100 chart, making it Switchfoot's fastest-selling album to date. The music finds songwriter Jon in a new place— world famous, rich, successful, yet more certain than ever that

Jerome *(left)* and newest Switchfoot member Andrew Shirley tune up for a performance on an Australian TV show. Andrew's musical influences include jazz musician Miles Davis, the Dave Matthews Band, and—essential for every Switchfoot member—U2.

fame and money don't provide the answers to life's biggest questions.

The first single, "Stars," tells the story of a lost and confused person who finds clarity and purpose in gazing at the stars. The groundbreaking video for the song was filmed partly underwater—so all the Switchfoot guys appear to be rocking out in zero gravity. The band members float several feet above the ground, seeming to cling to their microphones for dear life. When Jon opens his mouth to sing, bubbles come out.

Helped along by the creative video, "Stars" began climbing up the Billboard singles charts.

## The World of *Lowercase People*

An exciting new project by the band is called *Lowercase People*. Jon Foreman described it to MTV News as an "interactive online magazine for art, music, literature and international issues of social justice." Switchfoot aims to create a place for dialogue where the famous and not-so-famous will be able to discuss issues that are important to them. For Switchfoot, those issues might range from music to international aid for Africa. Each member will bring his or her own unique interests to the conversation.

Is Switchfoot here to stay? Will they be rock legends? Where will they be twenty years from now? Perhaps drummer Chad Butler summed it up best when he told an interviewer for the Web site musicOMH.com: "I think twenty years from now, we'll definitely be at the beach looking back at the years we were in a band. Surfing is sort of a lifestyle thing and it will stay with us forever. But music is what we are devoted to right now so we don't miss it [surfing] . . . We love doing music and nothing can take us away from doing this—it's the greatest job in the world."

# Timeline

**1996** Jon Foreman, Chad Butler, and Tim Foreman form Switchfoot. The band is offered a record deal by music producer Charlie Peacock.

**June 1997** Tim Foreman graduates from San Dieguito High School. The band releases its first album, *The Legend of Chin*.

**November 1998** The song "You" from *The Legend of Chin* is featured on the teen drama *Dawson's Creek*.

**2000** Jerome Fontamillas joins Switchfoot early in the year, playing with them in the recording sessions for their third album, *Learning to Breathe*.

**January 2001** Switchfoot receives a Grammy nomination for Best Rock Gospel Album.

**January 2002** The movie *A Walk to Remember* is released, featuring four Switchfoot songs and a duet with Jon Foreman and Mandy Moore.

**December 2002** Switchfoot is invited to the Nashville summit for DATA and meets U2's lead singer, Bono.

**December 2004** Switchfoot's fourth album, *The Beautiful Letdown*, is certified double platinum.

**September 2005** Switchfoot releases *Nothing Is Sound*, which debuts at number 3 on the Billboard album chart.

# Discography

*The Legend of Chin*, 1997, Re:Think

*New Way to Be Human*, 1999, Re:Think

*Learning to Breathe*, 2000, Re:Think

*A Walk to Remember* soundtrack, 2002, Sony

*The Beautiful Letdown*, 2003, Columbia Records

*The Early Years 1997–2000*, 2004, Sparrow

*Nothing Is Sound*, 2005, Columbia Records

## DVD

*Switchfootage*, 2003, available only at Switchfoot.com

*Live in San Diego*, 2004, Sony

*Feet Don't Fail Me Now*, 2005, available only at Switchfoot.com

# Glossary

**apathy**  A feeling of not caring about anything.

**Billboard charts**  The charts published by *Billboard* magazine that measure music sales and radio airplay.

**demo tape**  A first recording made by a band that does not have a recording contract. Its purpose is to convince record companies to offer a record deal or to convince concert venues to hire the band for live performances.

**genre**  A type or category; for example, gospel is a genre of music.

**marketing**  Helping to sell something, for example, by advertising.

**publicity**  Helping a band get on television and in the news, for example, by arranging interviews.

**rhythm guitarist**  The guitarist responsible for playing the rhythm or beat of a song, accompanying the lead guitarist.

**title track**  A song that has the same name as the album on which it appears.

**track**  Any song on an album.

**venue**  A place for a band to perform, such as a rock club or concert hall.

# For More Information

MTV Networks
1515 Broadway
New York, NY 10036
(212) 258-8000
Web site: http://www.mtv.com/
   bands/az/switchfoot/
   artist.jhtml

Switchfoot
c/o Sony BMG Music
   Entertainment, Inc.
550 Madison Avenue
New York, NY 10022
(212) 833-8000
Web site: http://www.
   switchfoot.com

## Web Sites

Due to the changing nature of Internet links, the Rosen Publishing Group, Inc., has developed an online list of Web sites related to the subject of this book. This site is updated regularly. Please use this link to access the list:

http://www.rosenlinks.com/
   cmtm/swit

# For Further Reading

Bogdanov, Vladimir, Chris Woodstra, and Stephen Thomas Erlewine, eds. *All Music Guide to Rock: The Definitive Guide to Rock, Pop, and Soul*. San Francisco, CA: Backbeat Books, 2002.

George-Warren, Holly, and Patricia Romanowski, eds. *The Rolling Stone Encyclopedia of Rock & Roll*. New York, NY: Fireside, 2001.

Hermes, Will, and Sia Michel, eds. *Spin: 20 Years of Alternative Music; Original Writing on Rock, Hip-Hop, Techno, and Beyond*. New York, NY: Three Rivers Press, 2005.

Joseph, Mark. *Faith, God, and Rock & Roll: How People of Faith Are Transforming American Popular Music*. Grand Rapids, MI: Baker Books, 2003.

Shirley, David. *The History of Rock and Roll*. New York, NY: Franklin Watts, 1997.

Stockman, Steve. *Walk On: The Spiritual Journey of U2*. Orlando, FL: Relevant, 2005.

Thompson, John J. *Raised by Wolves: The Story of Christian Rock & Roll*. Toronto, ON: ECW Press, 2000.

# Bibliography

Bansal, Vik. "Switchfoot: Riding the Wave." musicOMH.com. January 2005. Retrieved October 25, 2005 (http://www.musicomh.com/interviews/switchfoot.htm).

Gardner, Elysa. "Switchfoot Takes Giant Leaps." *USA Today*, June 6, 2004.

Hiatt, Brian. "Lords of the Ring." *Entertainment Weekly*, November 5, 2004.

Jesusfreakhideout.com. "Switchfoot Learns to Breathe." September 25, 2000. Retrieved October 26, 2005 (http://www.jesusfreakhideout.com/interviews/Switchfoot.asp).

Kendall, Steve. "Pull a Switchfoot." *Blender*, March 2004, p. 44.

Richard De La Font Agency. "Switchfoot Press Release." Retrieved October 26, 2005 (http://www.delafont.com/music_acts/switchfoot.htm).

"These Three Brand-New Acts Are Rockin' the New Year." *Christianity Today*. January/February 1998. Retrieved October 25, 2005 (http://www.christianitytoday.com/cl/8c4/8c4022.html).

Vox Online. "Stepping into Liquid: Switchfoot Are Ready to Ride the Wave." September 26, 2003. Retrieved October 25, 2005 (http://www.voxonline.com/alternative/switchfoot/).

# Index

# About the Author

Robert Zimmerman is a former songwriter, singer, and piano player who has performed with several underground rock bands in New Haven, Connecticut. He is currently working as an editor and writer in New York City.

## Photo Credits

**Designer:** Gene Mollica; **Editor:** Brian Belval
**Photo Researcher:** Gene Mollica